THE END OF NEOMA

TILDA ALMQVIST

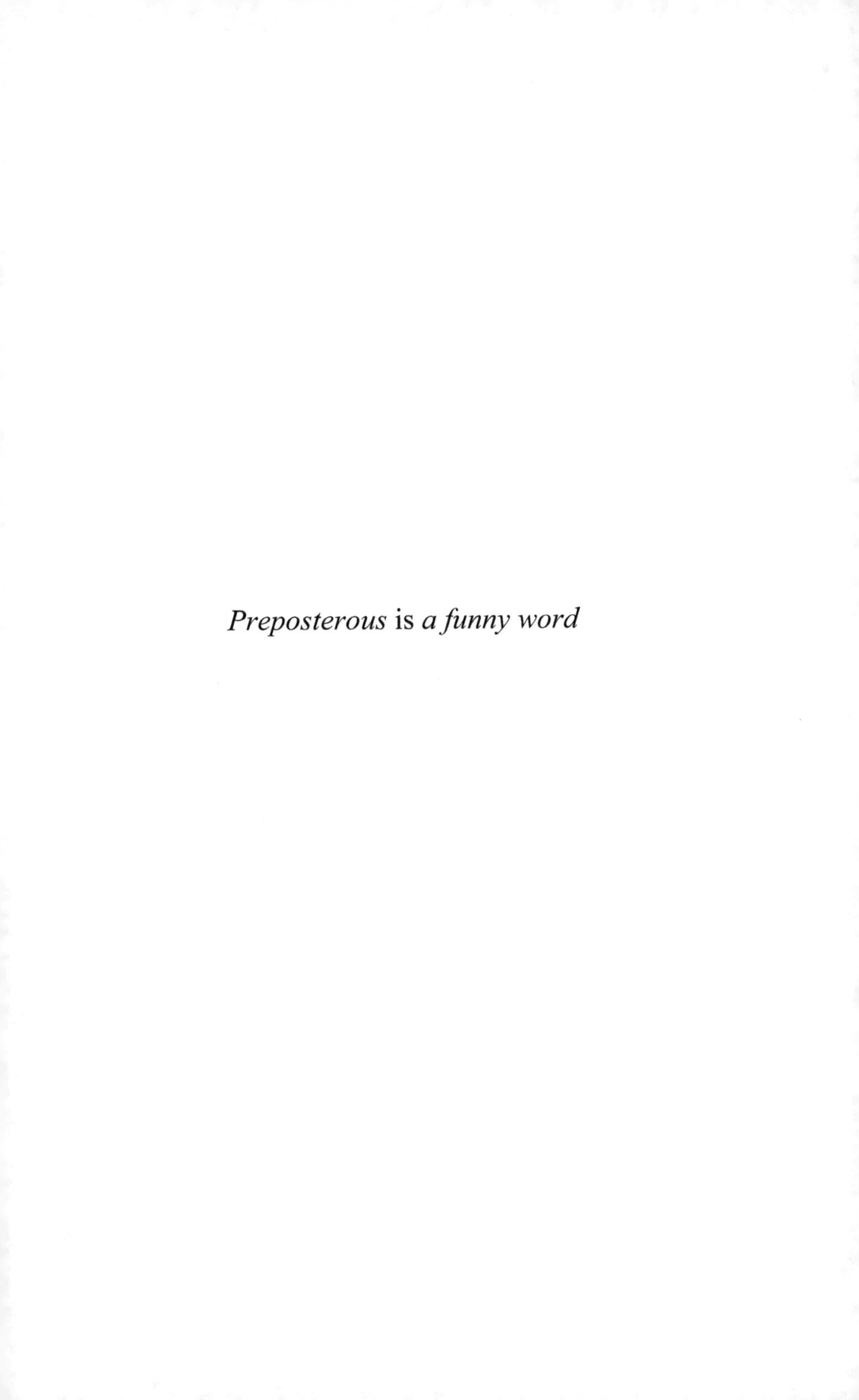

Preposterous is *a funny word*

EASTON

Neoma Galdur was insane.

At least according to Easton Keres, her husband, and the king of Calseeple. It was near humorous, she was the one to be born in the kingdom, as a princess, yet he held all the power. It was rare that he spoke of her as Neoma Keres, even though that was what she had been known as for well over a decade since they first got married. He was older, the marriage was arranged. Twenty years mattered far less when the previous king of Calseeple was desperate to gain an addition to the family fit for ruling, a man. Neoma was an only child at fifteen, with her father growing ever closer to his death bed, which might as well have been his grave. They were quick to have children, because that was what was expected, that was the point of their marriage, to create heirs. Unfortunately, they only managed to bring forth girls. There were two of them, two years apart. Praxidike was now fifteen, while Demanda was thirteen. Thankfully, Easton had little to no responsibilities related to the girls, just as his parents had him, he would let them deal with themselves.

While on the topic of siblings, as you might have understood by now, Easton was not an only child either. Growing up he often found himself disturbed by his younger brother, Eyal, something that had followed him into adulthood and had yet to leave him alone to this day. Eyal was a jealous person, always wishing for whatever his older brother had. Whether that be an object, a throne, or a person, he would try his very hardest to steal it for himself. But Easton's wife had never shown any interest in him, she hardly showed any interest in anything other than the children and her books. And that voice she always spoke of.

She never spoke about it directly, not to him, nor anyone for that matter. Only ever to herself, when she thought no one else was around to hear. She would stare at her reflection in the mirror, it was as if she was searching for something as she spoke in frustration, riddles, confusion. Confusion was certainly what she left Easton with after witnessing these 'conversations'. He had confronted her about it years ago. He was concerned about her wellbeing, her reaction to being questioned made it no better. She had grown immediately defensive, nearing aggression. She needed professional help.

Said professional help, however, would soon prove to be rather costly for the royal family. Doctor after doctor failed to provide with even the slightest of improvement, and still had to be paid their high rate for the job they *had* done. Which seemed to boil down to just showing up and watching the queen for a few hours as she was bored to death. But a failed attempt did not stop the king from trying, or two, or three, or so many that he had lost count. Unfortunately, these failures were noticeable. The kingdom's treasury was taking the greatest hit from all of these failures, Easton was annoyed and bothered, sure, Neoma was nothing but bored from all of the examinations, but the treasury grew… smaller. All of the money spent on doctors went faster than it came, it had to be made back somehow. Taxes were raised.

Calseeple was not much for trade, what they had in size they did not have in population. The majority of their land was taken up by forest no one wanted to chop down enough to expand into. The villagers they did have were not happy about the sudden increase in taxes, which would continue to grow, but there were not many other options. The Keres family were not born royals, rather they were born nobles with responsibility over a small section on the other side of the continent, the island Kuswaht. He had nothing else to lie back on, he knew good and well that if Eyal were to ever find out about the financial hardships of the kingdom, he would use it against him.

In recent months, Easton had taken to traveling further and further in search of someone who could finally fix whatever was wrong with his wife, or find a solution to the growing money problems. But there was not much luck to be found. That was until his advisor, Malachi, had found something that may be useful.

The red-haired man stumbled into the king's office, out of breath from moving with haste to reach the room. He clutched a leather-bound book against his chest, shutting the door with one big sigh. He looked over at the king, sitting at his desk with glasses perched on the tip of his nose, and bowed.

"My lord," Malachi said, taking the seat across from him after an approving nod.

"Did you run all the way here?" Easton asked, removing the glasses and setting them down on the desk next to the stack of papers he had been reading.

"As a matter of fact, yes" Malachi said, still panting. After a moment of catching his breath, he placed the book down in front of Easton.

Easton moved the stack of papers out of the way and pulled the book closer, squinting at the title. *"Delviann: Myths and Tales*? Is this a joke?" He looked back up at Malachi with an unimpressed look, an eyebrow cocked.

Malachi reached over the table and flipped the book open. He turned the pages as he spoke. "Most Delviann tales are rooted in truth, as with any, but these are the truest of them all." He found the page he had been looking for and tapped it with one finger, a satisfied smile on his face as he leaned back in his chair to let Easton take a closer look. The book was open on a tale titled *The Shadowman*, next to an illustration of a well-dressed man in all black, shadows pouring in and out of every crevasse, a wide-brimmed hat tilted down, keeping his face from being seen. Easton looked back up at Malachi, waiting for him to continue.

"He is known for making deals with people, for anything. You could ask him to fix Neoma's health issues *and* the financial difficulties."

"And you're certain of this?"

"As certain as I can be."

Easton only looked at him for a moment, pondering. His eyes traveled back down to the book, to the papers next to him, and finally back up to Malachi. Direct eye contact.

"Use anything you need from the remaining treasury to prepare for the trip and find me a good reason to go to Delviann." Easton pushed the book away and spread the stacked papers back out on the desk, turning his eyes away from the advisor. "I want this done as soon as possible, Malachi."

The advisor mumbled a response and stood, making his way out of the room and shutting the door softly behind him. It was time to get to work.

The most difficult part of the whole scheme would prove to be finding a reason for his travels. A random trip to Delviann would be sure to cause suspicion among the people, and Easton's brother. Everything was figured out within a few weeks. Any attainable information on the Shadow Man had been attained, an inn had been found, suitable for the king and close to the most popular area of Shadow Man tales and stories. That was the easy part.

He turned to the pile of unopened letters. Letters sent from all over the continent, even from *other* continents. Amid the pile was a sealed envelope from Delviann, recognizable from the light green tint of the paper. Using a letter opener, he tore open the envelope and extracted the letter. It was fairly recent, a month or two old. It was an invitation to a gathering with the Delvi court of monsters to attempt an alliance with Gloh. Some form of peace. And that was a perfectly good reason to travel to Delviann without raising any suspicion.

It was early in the morning, Easton was sitting inside of a moving carriage, traveling down to Kuswaht to board the ship that would take him across the waters to Delviann. His wife and children had been informed he would be spending the next few days away on a business trip, of which he had had many. The boat was set to leave in the early afternoon with a late arrival. He would travel to the inn Malachi had arranged for him and sleep for the night. Then, he would begin his search for the Shadow Man before had to attend the meeting with the court. Even though it was only a cover-up for the real reason for his visit. What could possibly go wrong?

The ride across the water was quiet as it could be, it was calming. He was mostly left alone aside from being approached by one of the crewmates abord the ship, who was soon to leave him be. Every now and then something could be spotted in the waters below them. What, exactly, may never be answered. Because frankly, Easton simply did not care about what may be inhabiting the waters, whether it be mermaids or krakens or regular salmon. His focus lay on his meeting to-be with the Shadow Man, and his curiosity with the meeting to-be with the Delvi court. Looking around him at the other travelers, he did not recognize anyone to be a representative from Gloh. He knew they did not have much in regards of riches to make them stand out much from others, but they remained unique in what they wore, having no access to imports. If what he knew of their hatred also stood true, they may not want to spend any more time in Delviann than needed, if they show at all.

Hours had passed before they boarded in the Devuthe docks, the sky had turned dark, and the air wrapped around them coldly. The inn he was to stay in was close enough to the docks for him to comfortably, enough, walk to even at such a late hour. It was a swift end to the night as no time was wasted in checking in and getting to his room. He could not be bothered to unpack the few articles of clothing he had brought for his stay, which he hoped would be as short as possible for the sake of his own sanity.

He slept late into the day, he had no other duties than his search for the Shadow Man and the meeting the following day. No matter when he had awoken, the plan had always been to remain in his room until after midday. More time for the pub to fill up. He had learned it was a good place to search for information on near any matter, the people there were buzzed at the very least. Chatty. Easton held his head high, confident, as he walked down the cobbled road. The inn was far behind him as he approached what he assumed to be the pub further down. From a distance he could only barely make out the sign hanging above the door. *The Iron Spider*. He considered the name odd, and as he stepped inside, he learned why. The first thing he was met with upon entry, was an iron spider roughly the size of his head, fastened the to the wall. He stared at it with an incredulous look on his face.

"Don't be too worried," a man called out from the bar. There was a subtle accent in his voice Easton couldn't place. "It ain't a real one."

He turned his head to see a fair-skinned man of similar age to himself. A wooden mug in hand.

"Is it based on a real one?" Easton asked, striding over to where the man sat, taking the seat a chair over.

"Supposed to be," he took a healthy sip from his mug. "Some sort of fear-sensing spider a couple ways over. No one knows what it does to you though."

"You know a lot about things like these?" He looked over at the man with a raised brow.

"I suppose I've been livin' around these parts to know a thing or two." He looked him over and extended his hand. "Harold, it's good to meet you."

Reluctantly, Easton extended his hand over to the man, Harold. "Easton," he said, hand clasping around the stranger's. They shook it once before letting go and returning to their own spaces. He did not seem to recognize him, or he did and simply didn't care. What did it matter? "I was wondering if you might know anything about this… Shadow Man I've been hearing of."

"You're not from these parts, are ya'?" He took another swig. "I believe the best place to go is Iron Wood, just past the border into Jehld. Ask and he shall come. That's what they say, anyway." Harold turned back to his drink, sensing correctly that the conversation was over.

Easton slid off the chair and stood, he offered the man a nod before making his way back over to the door, sparing the metal spider a final look before stepping back outside. The sun was further down on the sky as they entered early afternoon. The border between Devuhte and Jehld was not too far, but catching a carriage ride would certainly speed up the process of getting there. It brought him to one of several entrances to Iron Wood. Small people with wings on their backs, and translucent skin, hovered in the air around it as he approached. They did not speak nor approach, he walked inside of the woods, seeing nothing unusual. But surely, there must be.

He walked further, grey eyes scanning the trees surrounding him on every side. The trees looked like any other tree, tall, with sparse leaves. They weren't quite brown, there was a grey tone to them that rendered a closeness to metal. It was cold to the touch, hard. He did not know how far to walk. The entrance was out of sight, the man, Harold, had not been too specific with *where* in Iron Wood to go before attempting to make contact with the Shadow Man himself. He hoped this was good enough.

Easton cleared his throat, standing between two trees. "Shadow Man," he called out. His voice was just above average level. It was not a shout, but it traveled in the wind, being carried further and further until it stopped, and dropped. Maybe he was crazy now too… It felt as if he could see his words traveling in the wind, halting, falling down to the ground into a pile of shadows. The shadows twisted and folded on the ground, slowly rising and growing, forming into a silhouette of a man. And then he stood. The Shadow Man.

"Are you real?" Easton spoke after several moments of silence. He could not take his eyes off of the man made of shadows, he had watched him build himself from nothing into a full person. He looked just like the drawing from the book. Tall, well-dressed, face hidden beneath a wide-brimmed hat, all with shadows pooling in and out of every possible crevice.

The Shadow man chuckled at Easton's disbelief. He took a step closer, and another, and another. The distance between was growing narrower until they were at arm's length. He placed a shadow-covered hand on the king's shoulder. He seemed to smile. "I am as real as the problems of your life. The problems that led you to *me*." He took a small step back, letting go of Easton's shoulder. He extended his other hand out towards him. "I advise you to shake my hand."

Easton hesitated, his silver-tinted brows furrowing. Everything about what he was doing felt unreasonable. He had traveled away from his home to make yet another attempt at fixing his mad wife, but with each step he took to reach that goal it felt as if he was growing mad alongside her. He forced his arm to move upward, he forced his hand grasp that of the Shadow Man's. At first, he expected it to pass clean through, but there was substance hidden beneath the shadows. With their hand clasped together they shook it down once, and the surrounding area melted away into darkness, a void, then it reshaped itself into a room. The walls were covered in bookshelves holding books and scrolls, inks and quills. The only part of the walls not covered in shelves was the space carved out for a door.

The Shadow Man let go of Easton's hand and clapped him on the shoulder as he moved past him. "Easton Keres, was it?" He took a seat in a grand chair in front of a clean, wooden desk. "Take a seat."

Before Easton was able to fully turn his body around, an invisible force pushed him down into a wooden chair which swiveled around with only one leg touching the floor, so he faced the Shadow Man. A long piece of yellowed parchment flew off one of the shelves and landed cleanly on the desk, shortly followed by a vial of ink and a black quill. Easton watched on with wide eyes taking over his expression.

"If you would repeat to me what exactly you want done now, Easton," the Shadow Man said, "I can get yourself a contract."

"How the hell do you know my name?" Easton's eyes had narrowed into slits, eyeing the man of shadows in front of him with suspicion as he tapped the ink-soaked quill against the rim of the vial.

"The same way I know that the kingdom you married yourself into, Calseeple, is that correct? Is on the brink of bankruptcy, and the continuous increase in taxes to make up for the money spent trying to solve your wife's mental issues isn't sitting well with your people. Is that correct or did I miss something?" Easton did not speak, for he found no words no matter how far he searched in his mind. Perhaps he should have expected it, after all he had sought out the help of a mystical creature, *thing*. He should not be shocked that it knows what he is after. But what did he want in return for such a service? "I've finished up a contract for you," the Shadow Man said. Easton looked over at the parchment which was now covered in words detailing the deal he had asked to make; the Shadow Man must have used whatever magic he possessed to draft it up while he was lost in thought. "You sign at the bottom." The Shadow Man flipped the parchment around, so it faced Easton, placing the quill on the side of it.

"Are you trying to fool me?" Easton asked, looking up at the Shadow Man's hidden face. The words written on the parchment were small and close together, but not illegible, still, it would be a pain to read through even if you had the time. "What do you get out of this?"

"*You* get your riches returned to you," he extracted a small, round vial containing a translucent purple liquid, topped off with a cork, "and your wife has her sanity returned to her." He placed the vial on the desk. "*I* get a place to rest in your castle at my own demand." He raised one hand and adjusted his hat. "All you have to do is sign."

Easton reached for the quill. "So long as your wife drinks the potion, our contract stands," the Shadow Man continued. He held the quill still in his hand for a moment as he considered what he was about to do. It was easy. Was it too easy?

He brought the tip of the quill down to the paper, signing his signature in swooping letters. Then the deed was done. The Shadow Man tipped his hat and gestured towards the potion. Easton took it as the other man pulled the contract back into his grasp, yet again, the conversation was over, and with no other form of exiting the small room, Easton turned toward the door. He was relieved when the chair did not move for him this time and he was able to simply stand and move to the door himself, without intervention. The doorknob turned and the door opened, but there was nothing on the other side. It was the same darkness they had found themselves in before the room had appeared. He hesitated, the Shadow Man remained quiet, he stepped into the darkness. And, for a moment, that was all that surrounded him, then, just like before, it melted away and he stood back in the forest.

The sun was setting in the horizon, casting an orange glow over the trees. It had not felt like any more than ten minutes with the Shadow Man but based on the look of his surroundings it must have at least been a couple of hours. Easton turned in the direction of the entrance he had used and began walking, walking, walking until he made it out past the small creatures. They said nothing. There was no carriage he could ride as he walked further; he would have to walk the whole way back to the inn. It wasn't all too far, but far enough to make him dream for the bed that wasn't very soft in the room that wasn't very nice. Sleep, however, always had been, and always was.

Malachi had done his job and arranged for a private carriage to transport the king of Calseeple to the center district in order to attend the peace meeting with the Delvi court. He stepped inside the building in the very center of the circle that marked the meeting of all the regions that made up Delviann. It was several stories high with tall windows on every level, but he could not see inside.

Easton pushed the door open with one hand, he had expected it to be pulled. Inside, he was met by a woman who was quick to approach him. She asked if he was here for the meeting, which he was. She looked relieved to see him there, recognizing the fact that he was from Kleurstark, specifically Calseeple. She led him out of the entry room and into a winding hallway. They passed several doors before stopping in front of a door seemingly made from stone. The woman who had led him there bowed her head and walked away, leaving Easton alone in front of the grand door. He *pushed* the door open and stepped inside a round room filled with people. At least a dozen people milled around a circular table, chatting, and standing off on their own. At first glance, majority of them looked to be human. But as he looked closer, small details stuck out. A pair of sharp teeth in a smiling mouth, a pointy ear sticking out from someone's hair, scales on hands. It became clear they were, very much not, human. One of the Delvi who was stood near the table speaking to what he believed to be an elf, based on the pointed ear, spotted him and quickly concluded their conversation, and approached him with a friendly smile on their face. It was then he realized that the person approaching him was not so subtly Delvi as the others were. Spilling out of their sleeves were brown feathers, their eyes were a bright, deep orange that took up nearly the entirety of their almond eyes. His limited knowledge of the different Delvi kinds led to him being unable to identify what this was. However, they appeared friendly enough.

"You're one of the rulers from Kleurstark? I believe your name is Easton?" they said, clasping their hand together. They had long nails resembling the claws of a bird, a light-yellow tint in color. Easton nodded. "Normally we don't have any Kleurstark representatives in attendance." They clapped their hands together, eyes wide with a cheeky smile on their face. "I completely forgot to introduce myself, I'm a complete stranger to you. So sorry about that. I should probably do that before we actually start whenever the Gloh representatives show. I'm Yumao," they extended a hand, "it's nice to meet you."

Easton looked down at their claw-ridden hand, then back up at their slim face, orange almond-eyes staring at him with a gentle expression. But he had not traveled all the way here to be rude at a meeting he had no prior intention to attend. He clasped his hand in theirs, put on a polite smile, and shook their hand. They let go just when the door opened for a second time, making room for two above-averagely dressed people, a man and a woman, arms hooked. They were not quite dressed in the ways of a noble, but not quite a peasant either, some sort of combination of the two to still show a certain status with what was available to them in their small region. Yumao bowed their head to Easton and walked away, rejoining the elf they had previously spoken with.

A woman who appeared to be not much older than Easton stepped forward from the crowd, hair the color of strawberry blonde with a snow-white creeping up from the tips. She wore a long dress layered with thread and vine, reaching down to her feet, sleeves going from opaque to layers of leaves at her wrists. The foundation layer of the dress reminded him of a leaf covered in frost in the midst of winter.

"We thank you for gracing us with your presence, Sampson, Edith," the elf said. "It has been long awaited."

The couple scanned the room with an ugly expression of disgust and disdain. "You won't mind if we stand by the door, wouldn't want to *catch anything* from being too close to *your* kind," the man, Sampson said. Easton watched on with an eyebrow raised as the woman, Edith covered her nose and mouth with her hand for a moment.

"I don't understand how anyone could stand this place, everything is just so… *disgusting* and *unnatural*," she scowled, fixing her sleeve at her wrist.

The elf inhaled through her nostrils. "I am sure you know why we asked you to come here today, yes?"

"Well, we're hoping you've found a way to rid yourselves of all of those *problems* you have so you can finally become normal," Sampson said, "then there will be no problem and these little visits will no longer be necessary."

"It almost feels like you're trying to accuse *us* of being the problem here, always making *us* come *here*, rather than the other way around. Is that what you're trying to say?" Edith added.

"We are not trying to accuse you of anything, we are simply trying to find some form of middle ground to bury the hatchet," the elf said. "The goal is to move past the past."

"How are we meant to move past anything when the problem is still glaringly obvious. We are surrounded with people covered in feathers, and fangs, and pointy ears, and you want us to move past that?" Sampson exclaimed. He spoke in such a way that clearly carried through his shock at the apparent audacity the Delvi were showing him and his wife. With how small the region was, and how isolated they preferred to be, he wondered how he had met his wife.

"This is just preposterous," Edith complained, tightening her grip on her husband's arm, nose upturned.

Sampson scoffed and turned on his heel, Edith in tow. They pulled the doors open and stepped out, leaving the room of Delvi monsters, and Easton in varying stages of emotion. Majority of the room felt a heavy disappointment at yet another failed peace attempt, Easton was struck with confusion. He did not bother with keeping up with the relationship issues between other regions, he knew things had not been good between Gloh and Delviann after the attempted attack, but he was not aware it was quite this bad. He looked up to see Yumao casting him a sympathetic look and a sad smile, he bowed his head in return and made an exit himself. The meeting appeared to be over, he was not the first to leave following the Gloh representatives.

He had reached the end of his trip to Delviann, it had not been long-lasting, but it had been plentiful. Tales of his meeting with the Shadow Man was not something he could share back at home, but his daughters might appreciate hearing of Yumao the siren. After collecting together his things at the inn, he headed back to the docks where he was able to catch a late ship. He would be back in Calseeple in the afternoon of the following day.

Neoma Galdur would soon no longer be insane.

NEOMA

Neoma's life was far from ordinary.

It wasn't an unpreferred circumstance in her eyes. Mysteries and riddles were something she often turned to when it felt as if time was moving slower than usual. If she were not to be allowed to assist in the mysteries of her kingdom, then she would find some of her own. Though she never expected for one of them to be in the very center of her life. The daily routine of a queen was nothing unusual or unexpected, the majority of the duties required from the royal family were performed by her husband, Easton, and she took care of her daughters when needed. It was not often they needed her help, but she enjoyed the time they spent together. Even with the voice that never seemed to reach her. It sounded far away, muffled as if in another room or underwater. This mystery proved to be much more difficult to solve, but it wasn't the only complication in her life. There were several instances before everything truly became a mystery that remains unsolved.

The sun shone brightly down on the pair as they walked through the grass, leaving imprints of their shoeless feet behind them. The mother and daughter had abandoned their shoes by the road where the carriage waited to return to the castle. The horses were kept in place by the coachman who steered them while the two members of the royal family enjoyed their time basking in the sun.

Neoma had asked earlier in the day whether Praxidike and Demanda wished to join her on a trek down to the river; only Praxidike, the older of the two, had said yes. Together they danced and sang with their bare feet in the grass, dew from the early morning latching onto their exposed skin. The girl spun around on the grass with her arms wrapped around herself in a tight hug, her dark hair swung loose around her. She began to haphazardly sing the words of the lullaby Neoma always sang to her before bed, continuously interrupted by bouts of laughter. Soon, the mother joined in as well with a beautiful voice and thus creating a beautiful memory between mother and daughter.

"Watch the fire burn now," Neoma sang to the sky above her, twirling in the grass as she did, the skirt of her dress wrapping around her legs. Praxidike joined her every other word but was soon distracted by something else. "Let the ice run cold," she continued.

Praxidike turned her attention fully towards her mother and stretched out her hands for Neoma to take. Hand in hand the two continued to sing and dance with the sounds of trees rustling in the wind and birds chirping. "Orange like a flower, watch my eyes glow."

The laughter continued between the lines, resulting in frequent breaks within the song. Praxidike let go of her mother's hand shortly after taking them to continue her dance and sing along. Only growing quiet and still as a blue bird sat in a tree across the river caught her attention. Neoma continued to sing, not acknowledging the bird. "Don't run away now, don't be so scared." And she continued to twirl. "I'm a pretty flower, why-" The peace was soon interrupted, and Neoma stopped dead in her tracks, a pit forming in her stomach at the sound of a soft thud and the scream of her daughter. She felt a tingle at her fingertips as she rushed to Praxidike's side.

"Mom!" Praxidike cried, bringing her arms close and fidgeting her hands without taking her eyes off the tree line. Neoma wrapped her arms around her and kissed her head, repeatedly asking what had happened. When she was provided with no response her eyes followed Praxidike's.

The bird no longer sat on a branch across the river, it was now lying lifeless on the ground. Spots were charred black from burns, while others were white and covered with ice. Neoma stroked Praxidike's hair and pushed an equally dark strand of her own behind her ear as she leaned down.

"It's okay, Praxidike," she said. "It's all going to be okay. Just go back to the carriage and we'll go home." A sniffle and a short hug was the only form of response from Praxidike before she let go and ran over to where the carriage awaited them. Neoma watched as she climbed inside before turning her attention over to the feathered corpse, stepping as close to it as possible without stepping in the river itself. She crouched down without taking her eyes off of the soulless white bead.

"Say something," Neoma whispered. An orange ring played at the edge of her iris. "Speak to me," she spat out in a whisper loud enough that it was almost her regular voice. A quick glance behind her confirmed that neither the coachman nor her daughter had heard. It was clear the bird was not going to provide her with anything useful, accepting defeat she joined her daughter in the carriage, and they were on their way back to the castle. Neoma wiped the stray tears off of her daughter's face as the carriage rolled down the path, hitting the occasional rock. She made her promise not to tell anyone, not her father, not her sister. It would be their little secret. One of many.

More moments like it arose over the years. More secrets to be kept. The most important detail was always to make sure that Easton never found out. Secrets involving Praxidike, secrets involving Demanda, secrets involving them both. The voice far away continued to speak, there were times when it felt as if it were coming closer, but it always backed away again. She swore she could hear it whisper underneath the surface of the water that winter. It was a couple of years after the bird had died, Praxidike was twelve, Demanda was ten. The two of them were outside ice skating on the frozen pond. The ice was thin in spots, thin enough to break under the pressure of a young girl. Praxidike fell through while Demanda stood on the edge of the water. Neoma walked outside right as it happened, as the weak spot in the ice caved in and pulled Praxidike below the surface of the cold water. She broke into a run, only slowing down once she reached the ice. She lay her body down on the ice and stuck her hands into the water, frantically trying to grasp her daughter's hands. There was booming pain in her skull, it felt as if it was going to cave in on itself when she saw a glimpse of green seconds before Praxidike's hands grasped hers. And the pain was gone.

An hour later Praxidike was seated on Neoma's lap inside of the queen's chambers. Neoma had an arm wrapped around her stomach while the other stroked her hair. Her hair and clothes were dry, and she was no longer shivering, hopefully she would be able to avoid any sickness from the previous drop in temperature. Luckily, Neoma had been gifted with her father's orange magic and was therefore able to quickly solve the problem. Praxidike would be too distracted to understand what she was doing and Demanda had been instructed to wait outside. Neither of the girls had begun showing any signs of magic, maybe the gene had skipped a generation. Perhaps that was a good thing. They were lucky this time, fortunately Easton had left for a trip a few days prior, it meant he would never hear of the accident. He had never liked magic.

"Mom?" Demanda called out from the other side of the chamber door.

"You can come in now, darling."

The large wooden door creaked open slowly, allowing enough space for Demanda to slip into the room before it swung shut behind her. She walked up to her mother and sister and took a seat beside them, leaning her head on Neoma's shoulder.

"Let's make this our special little secret," Neoma said.

Those weren't the only secrets kept over the years, but they were the most notable ones. Things had been going well for a long time, and all things that go up must go back down. It's a matter of balance, bad events being considered as good due to lack of consequences must be equalized for the balance to remain nice and even. After an additional three years it was time to enact a consequence great enough to restore the balance to its original standing.

Neoma stood leaned against the wall outside of her husband's, the King's office, twirling a lock of dark hair around her finger. The door was open just enough so that the conversation occurring inside could be heard but not enough for any eavesdropper to be spotted. Easton's personal advisor and close friend had returned from a trip into the neighboring kingdom of Gortasia a couple of hours prior. He had been quick to swift him away and had requested utmost privacy. He couldn't even close the door properly, and he had the nerve to call her mad.

"The other nobles have been talking, my lord," the advisor, Malachi, said.

"It's nothing but gossip," Easton spat, not even bothering to cover up the annoyance in his voice. Noble gossip traveled far and fast, he may have attempted to brush it off but it was a concern. If enough people agree on something it becomes the truth. "Let them speak."

"They've picked up on her behavior," Malachi continued. "Speaking to mirrors, to the moon, staring at shadows. They are saying that she has gone mad." It was quiet for a moment as neither of them spoke. One of them sighed, most likely Malachi. "We both know there is truth in what is being spread. She has been acting this way for years, speaking to nothing, luck has been on our side that it hasn't been spoken of by others until now."

"And what do you suggest I do?" Easton said, his voice calmer, quieter. Neoma almost had to lean in closer to hear him speak.

"I can't tell you that, Easton," Malachi said. "I suggest we should keep an eye on her, look for signs to see if it's getting any worse. If it is, perhaps…"

"If it gets worse, we take action." She could hear one of the men stepping close to the door and instinctively took a step away herself. Knowing the conversation was coming to end she could no longer risk listening in case of being caught. A servant would pay her no mind, perhaps make her the topic of conversation in the kitchens, but Easton would have a word or two for her. She walked down the hall at a calm pace, stopping only at the stairs to catch the last of the conversation.

"And if they keep talking?"

"We give them something else to talk about."

With hurried steps she walked down the stairs, smoothing down the front of her dress as she heard the door fall closed with a gentle thud. She continued through the halls until she reached the front door where she stopped a passing servant, asking her if she could please fetch her cloak. Neoma faced the door as she waited for the servant to return, pretending not to hear the footsteps growing louder as they walked in her direction. Easton. There was something interesting in developing the ability to tell a person apart by the sound of their footsteps alone, though it wasn't always all that useful.

"Neoma," he said, stopping to stand a respectable distance behind her. Taking a deep breath and stopping herself from rolling her eyes at the interruption, she turned around to face her husband. "Where are you headed?"

"The cemetery," she said. "To pay my respects to Dolores, and my mother and father, like I do every week." Technically it wasn't a lie. She did visit the cemetery every week and yet to do it, it wasn't her intended location, but it was close enough to it that she could stop by before returning home. By this point, the servant had returned and handed over her deep blue cloak with a bow before returning to her other duties. Neoma swung it around her shoulders and clasped it in the front and looked up at Easton. "I'll join you and the children for dinner in the evening." Without waiting for a response or dismissal, she pulled the large castle doors open and stepped outside, leaving Easton alone in the hall.

The air stung colder as the horse trotted down the dirt path that would lead her into the heart of the forest. How come witches always lived in the forest? Perhaps it was about putting distance between them and the village people, they weren't always such big fans of witches, or maybe it was just a preference for nature. Either way, the witch she knew was always accessible through the forest. Blanche Servius was her name, she referred to the entrances as windows, entrances that could be used from different locations but all leading to the same place. Neoma didn't entirely understand how it all worked but she didn't need to, that's not why she was going to see her. She reached the usual spot where Blanche would leave her door and tied her horse to a tree, all while scanning her surroundings for the old wooden door that led into the witch's home. It stood in the middle of a small clearing near the end of the main path. She walked up to it and knocked three times as she always did, as she was instructed to do near the beginning of their friendship, before opening the door and stepping inside.

"Blanche?" Neoma called out into the empty room as she shut the door behind her. She could hear a commotion from one of the backrooms and a string of silent curses soon followed. Before long, Blanche entered the room with a smile on her face as she approached Neoma with open arms. The two enveloped in a hug.

"Neoma," Blanche said, pulling away from the hug, her blonde curls brushing against Neoma's cheek. "What can I do for you?"

"I believe the girls are old enough."

There was a pause. "Are you sure?"

Neoma nodded. Blanche nodded and walked over to the far wall of the room, grabbing a vial of yellow liquid off of a shelf, followed by a jar of dried flower petals.

The ingredients lightly clinked together as she placed them down on the table in the middle of the room.

"The process of giving you a new life requires two separate potions," Blanche explained as she continued to grab and measure odd liquids and materials. "One now, and one in a couple of months. The one I am making for you now will stop your aging, the second one will build off of that to reshape your life." After having finished speaking Blanche walked over to a large indent in the wall where a pile of burnt sticks lay with a cauldron hung above it. With a flick of her finger the sticks were set ablaze, the high flames surrounded the bottom of the cauldron, changing the color from a deep black to a glowing orange. Neoma walked closer as the various ingredients were thrown into the now boiling water. Three drops of the orange liquid, six dried flower petals, and so it continued. Once everything had been added and stirred together with a large stick the water had reduced and changed into a thick black potion. Blanche tilted the cauldron down, allowing for the newly brewed concoction to be poured into a pear-shaped vial without leaving a single drop behind.

"Should I be worried about the color?" Neoma asked as Blanche placed a cork into the bottle.

She answered with a sly smile. "Not too much." The bottle was warm to the couch, the liquid inside barely moving as Neoma gingerly slid it into the pocket of her dress.

The women exchanged their goodbyes and shared a hug before the queen returned outside into the cluster of trees. Following the path, she relocated her steed and returned home, making sure to stop by the cemetery. She had no intention of lying to her husband, even if she didn't have much care for his opinion of her. The ride home was quicker, aside from the additional stop, the sky had darkened in the time spent with Blanche which meant that dinner would soon be deserved. She had promised to join Easton and the girls, she could drink the potion afterwards.

As usual dinner had consisted mainly of Praxidike and Demanda sharing details about their day, it was either instigated by Neoma or brought up by them. She made sure to listen closely to every word they said, respond, and smile. She knew she was going to miss them, but this had been her entire life. Always following directions and never being given a chance to live for herself. Maybe it was selfish, but she always did things for others, always lived for them, she deserved to be selfish.

Neoma was seated in front of her mirror, where she would sit every morning before getting dressed. She wondered if her face would change. Would her dark hair turn blonde? Or her blue eyes brown? The true effect the combined potions would have on her hadn't really been explained, not that she had asked. So it was her fault, really. What she had been told was to drink the immortality potion with tea. After dinner Neoma had asked for a teacup with cold water to be sent up to her chambers. It wasn't an unusual ask, she enjoyed heating the water herself since she was rarely given an opportunity to use her magic otherwise.

She drank the dark potion-infused tea without taking her eyes off of her reflection. "Do you have a name?" she asked the mirror. The voice didn't feel quite so distant today, she wanted to talk to it. She wanted it to answer. She took a long sip of her tea.

"Do you have magic? Of course, you do." She chuckled. "I've seen it before. But I can't tell what kind it is, could you tell me?"

She continued asking questions, but the voice continued to leave her on hold. Her hand wrapped tighter around the emptying teacup at every unanswered question, leaving a slight shake in her hand. She could feel the heat building up around her eyes, she knew it meant her magic was growing active but didn't stop. She wanted an answer. The only one she was given was a ruined and frosted over mirror and a confused child. Neoma let out a silent curse, Praxidike was standing outside of her door.

And so, it continued. The other nobles never stopped talking, because in their eyes Neoma only grew madder, practically confirming their suspicions. She was often spotted speaking to mirrors, usually her reflection but looking at it so intensely as if searching for something deep inside of it. They would often be found in shards on the floor shortly after. She also spoke to shadows at times, angry whispers of accusations could be thrown at the shadow of whoever was unfortunate enough to be passing her during one of these times. The moon also appeared to be a favorite of hers. However, she spoke to it differently. When Praxidike and Demanda were younger, Neoma would tell them stories of the moon. She had inherited her magic from her father who believed it to be a gift from the moon itself, everyone had different beliefs regarding the origin of the magic, but she believed in it too.

But it wasn't until late one evening, three months after Neoma's visit to Blanche, that everything fell apart, and the balance was restored. By this point the second and final potion had been finished. One of the guards, the one who had first introduced Neoma to the Servius witch, had personally delivered it to her that very morning. But every potion has its rules. In order for the potion to work properly and the spell to work, it had to be drunk directly from the bottle under the light of the full moon. Unlike the immortality potion, this was not to be mixed with anything, and the full moon's glow would be the final ingredient it needed to be activated. Neoma was on her way to drink the potion out on the balcony but first she had agreed to walk Praxidike to her chambers before bed. Following the same routine, Neoma stopped at one of the mirror's hung in the hall. As expected, it gave no response. The voice never did. She could feel the heat grow behind her eyes and for a brief moment they glowed orange with magic. The built-up heat spread onto the mirror which began to crack as the temperature grew inside of it, once it could no longer handle the immense heat the shards broke free of the frame and flew into the hall. Fortunately, there were no serious injuries caused by this outbreak aside from a small cut on Praxidike's cheek. Neoma's heartbeat rose as she saw the horrified look on her daughter's face and racing breath as a small drop of blood ran down her cheek. Easton reacted differently. Emotions always looked heightened on a person with an expressive face. Therefore, anger was not the right word to describe the feelings portrayed on the face of the king.

"What did you do?" he yelled. He rushed towards them and pulled Praxidike close, examining her face before turning to Neoma with a look of disgust added onto the preexisting anger caused by the situation. It was quite a scene to return to after his three-day trip. "You witch! Do you have no heart? Hurting your own child like this is...," he paused for a moment, scanning her face as he searched for the right words, "it's something only a demon would do. Malachi!"

His trusted advisor was quick to arrive along with a handful of guards, having seemingly been right around the corner. Malachi was quick to assess the situation, not that it would be difficult to guess what had happened based on the state of the people before him. He turned towards the guards behind him and nodded towards Neoma. The guards accepted their assignment without question and surged towards their queen. Her already fast beating heart only grew faster, her magic had hidden away inside of her, and she lacked any physical advantage. That's when she heard it.

"Hello," an airy voice said with a laugh. Neoma's eyes grew wide in surprise. It had talked, the voice always so far away was right beside her. Her open eyes quickly wanted to shut as a small ring of smoke appeared directly in front of them. A red ring to make them all believe her magic was more powerful than them. But it didn't stop them for long, because she did not possess the magic the voice had fooled them into thinking she had. It was no help. So, they seized her and dragged her away down the hall, all the while she was kicking and screaming. And she continued to do so the entire journey, until she was locked away in a tower, until she lost her voice.

DEMANDA

Demanda did not miss her mother.

It had been less than twenty-four hours since Neoma had been carried away to God-knows-where after harming Demanda's older sister. It had been an accident, of course, but it stirred enough worry for her removal to be the most reasonable option. She did not know where she was taken, Praxidike did not know, Easton probably did know. But he would not tell them such a thing. She and Praxidike had slept in Praxidike's bed that night after the wound on her cheekbone had been tended to. Easton had tucked them in, told them of a siren covered with feathers and bright orange eyes named Yumao he had met on his trip. He told them things were going to be okay.

Demanda smoothed down her nice dress, she stood outside of her father's office with the door open just enough for her to hear what they were saying inside. The king and his advisor, Easton and Malachi.

"I don't quite understand what it is you want done with her," Malachi said.

"Just follow through with what I told you," Easton said. "I want someone posted at all times, let things play out as they will." He sighed. "If you could go find Praxidike for me, make sure she is okay and ready for the announcement."

She could hear the shuffling of feet moving around inside the room, steadily approaching the door. Before she registered the need to move, the door opened and she made direct eye contact with Malachi, hands clasped together behind her back. Malachi turns his head back inside the room and clears his throat, nodding down at Demanda before walking away to find Praxidike. She was probably still in her room. Praxidike missed her mother.

Easton came out through the gap in the door, closing it slightly before kneeling down to Demanda's eye level. Her hands were now at her sides, her father grabbing them in his, their grey eyes meeting.

"How are you doing today, Demanda?" he asked.

"What were you talking about?" Demanda inquired, ignoring the question her father had asked.

Easton looked over his shoulder, into his empty office, recalling his conversation with Malachi. He turned back to Demanda. "It's nothing to worry about, Demanda. Let's go find your sister and Malachi."

The king stood up straight and pulled the door to the office closed, he extended his hand down towards his daughter who took with a somber smile on her face. Together they walked through the halls until they reached the grand balcony on the second floor where Malachi and Praxidike stood waiting by the glass doors. He extended his other hand to Praxidike, and together they walked out onto the edge of the balcony. Down below on the castle grounds stood a large crowd consisting of the villagers from around the kingdom. They had wanted to relay the announcement of the queen's fate as soon as possible, even if it meant news might travel slowly due to the fact not everyone would be able to make it on such short notice.

"People of Calseeple," Easton's voice boomed out over the crowd, loud and large. "I am sad to say I have asked you here today with unfortunate news. Your queen and mine, Neoma Keres, passed," there was a short pause, "late last night. She had been sick for some time, putting on a strong front as to not worry our beloved kingdom. But life is a cruel thing, and the heavens took her early. You may see less of me and my family in the time going forward as we adjust to this new reality; we will mourn as will you. We thank you for your time here today, may she rest in peace."

A murmur broke out into the crowd, but the royal family paid it no mind as they walked back inside the castle. Easton and his daughters were no longer holding hands, each breaking off on their own. Easton stroked his children on their heads before walking away with Malachi, Praxidike took a seat in a chair against the wall and just breathed, Demanda, she walked down the hall towards the royal quarters. Specifically, her mother's.

The room felt emptier than it ever had before. Each time she had gone there prior to her mother's supposed death, there had been something off about it. A certain coldness, a lack of recognition or safety she couldn't quite place correctly.

There had been to speak of what would happen to all of her mother's belongings following the event, but she figured that if there was anything *secret* to be found it might not be kept, and it certainly would not be given to neither her nor Praxidike. So, she was the first to search the room for anything peculiar she might have an interest in. There had been a lot of secrets kept between her, her sister, and her mother over the years. Plenty of things that felt less than natural. That's what she wished to find, but any other keepsake would be good too.

Her eyes flitted towards the vanity where a white quill lay, unused. Her mother had treasured that quill, vowing to never use it because it was too special. She had bought it many years ago at the queen's market, the first she had ever attended. That was when she met Dolores for the first time, when she made her first proper friend since her marriage to Easton. Demanda wanted it. And she would have it. But first, she peeked in the drawers of the vanity, inside the closet, under the bed. There, she found a book. It was wrapped in dark orange leather, silver lettering pressed into the cover spelled out *Magic of Color: Volume II*. She would take this too. Happy enough, she grabbed the belongings and made it back to her quarters unnoticed by anyone. The book would not be missed, it had been hidden away underneath her bed, after all. And as for the quill, she could whine that she wished to keep something that reminded her of her mother and there would be no problem.

The remainder of the day was spent with her nose in a book, *the* book. It was quite informative. Everything began to make sense regarding her mother. She had last seen her mother being taken away, dragged down the hall by guards with Malachi in tow, then she saw Easton consoling Praxidike with a bleeding cheek. All he had told her was that Neoma had hurt her. The two of them then left to patch up the small wound, leaving Demanda in the hall to find an answer to her own question. She found the broken mirror; it was not the first. Her mother had orange magic, thermal control as the book had described it, *that* was how all of those mirrors had been cracked and broken.

Magic was genetic. The tingle she felt inside of her chest, at the tips of her fingertips, the warmth. Her eyes changing color as she looked up at herself in the mirror.

They glowed like a fire.

THE SHADOW MAN

Yet another deal broken.

Easton Keres had failed to uphold his end of the contract he had signed during his visit to Iron Wood. He had agreed to give his wife, Neoma, a potion to clear her mind of troubles, and, in his opinion, return her sanity. That was the requirement. Give her the potion and Calseeple would not need to spend any more money on finding doctors, and all the money spent would be earned back in a fast manner, the people's taxes could be lowered, and they would no longer grow resentful of their rulers. For such a favor, Easton would provide the Shadow Man with a room in his castle to be used at his own will. It was not easy to expand business past the borders of Delviann. For one, not many knew of him in those parts. Tales of his business were a large part of Delviann where stories and legends thrived because they all carried large seeds of truth, making them much more believable than your typical bedtime story. For two, even if they did know of him, they would need to travel across the waters in order to meet with him. The Shadow Man's home was in Delviann with at least one place of rest in each region, and windows in several notable spots, such as Iron Wood.

But another broken contract was another broken contract, there was no need for the Shadow Man to take action, poor Easton Keres had enough problems as it was, and they would take care of it in a few years' time. If only he had given her that potion, things would have turned out very differently.

Acknowledgements

To start this one off I want to directly call out Zero, who has been my beta reader for a while now. I also want to call out their friend for the same reason. I would like to share some quotes that followed me sharing the cover for this.

"I have never been one for fictional men, but like..."

"I don't trust your judgement on this, I need a second opinion."

Zero then proceeded to send the picture of the cover to their friend.

"Hot. Would get f*cked by. He might not have a d*ck but he can hold things."

With that said, you both have problems, you stand no chance, give up now for your own good. Secondly, I would like to offer a thank you to my English 7 teacher who complimented Neoma's perspective which I originally wrote for a creative writing assignment and told me to continue writing. You may be able to notice that I did, and I hope you were not too disturbed by the weirdness of my friend.

And if you are one of those people who like the Shadow Man, or have the hots for him, he will be back. And Zero might have written a fanfic about him, who knows.